SKATES ON!

Written by Catherine Coe
Illustrated by Ceej Rowland

RISING ★ STARS

Hachette UK's policy is to use papers that are natural, renewable and recyclable products and made from wood grown in well-managed forests and other controlled sources. The logging and manufacturing processes are expected to conform to the environmental regulations of the country of origin.

ISBN: 9781398325388

Text, Illustrations, design and layout © Hodder and Stoughton Ltd
First published in 2021 by Hodder & Stoughton Limited (for its Rising Stars imprint, part of the Hodder Education Group),
An Hachette UK Company
Carmelite House, 50 Victoria Embankment, London EC4Y 0DZ

www.risingstars-uk.com

Impression number 10 9 8 7 6 5 4 3 2 1
Year 2025 2024 2023 2022 2021

Author: Catherine Coe
Series Editor: Tony Bradman
Commissioning Editor: Hamish Baxter
Illustrator: Ceej Rowland/Bright Group International
Educational Reviewer: Helen Marron
Design concept and layouts: Peter Banks
Editor: Amy Tyrer

With thanks to the schools that took part in the development of Reading Planet KS2, including: Ancaster CE Primary School, Ancaster; Downsway Primary School, Reading; Ferry Lane Primary School, London; Foxborough Primary School, Slough; Griffin Park Primary School, Blackburn; St Barnabas CE First & Middle School, Pershore; Tranmoor Primary School, Doncaster; and Wilton CE Primary School, Wilton.

A catalogue record for this title is available from the British Library.

Printed in the United Kingdom.

Orders: Please contact Hachette UK Distribution, Hely Hutchinson Centre, Milton Road, Didcot, Oxfordshire, OX11 7HH.
Telephone: (44) 01235 400555. Email: primary@hachette.co.uk

MIX
Paper from
responsible sources
FSC™ C104740

CONTENTS

CHAPTER 1

Joseph chased the football across the ground, but the striker got there first and booted it into the back of the net. All around him, Joseph's team groaned. He put his head in his hands. Why was he so bad at football?

"Sorry," Joseph said to Jake as he passed him, but Jake didn't even reply. Jake had been his best mate for years. He hardly spoke to him these days.

Joseph's team kicked off, but nobody passed the ball close to him. He was glad. At least then he couldn't make a mistake.

But then they lost the ball and had to defend. A winger ran towards Joseph and hit a pass to their striker. Joseph stuck his foot out to stop the ball. It flicked up ... and over the top of the goalkeeper into the back of the net for an own goal.

"Wow, you are on fire today, Joseph," joked the goalkeeper, Philippa.

"Sorry," Joseph said again. He couldn't believe he'd scored an own goal!
No wonder everyone teased him for being rubbish at football.

*

That weekend, Joseph stayed at his cousin's while his mum was at work. Luckily, Simone didn't play football. But she did play roller hockey. And she really wanted Joseph to join in with training that morning.

He was bound to be just as bad at roller hockey as he was at football. He'd never even heard of it!

"I'll just sit and cheer you on," Joseph said. "I don't mind."

So Joseph sat on the sidelines as Simone played roller hockey.

It looked like a lot of fun – Simone didn't stop grinning, even when she fell over. It was fast, too – the players rocketed over the rink, almost blurs. But Joseph wasn't going to play. He didn't want the roller hockey kids to make jokes about him like everyone at football did. No, it was much better to just sit on the side ... That way, he couldn't make himself look silly.

*

The next Saturday, Joseph's mum was working again, so Joseph was back at Simone's house.

This time, Simone pestered him to give roller hockey a go from the moment he arrived at the door.

"Why not try it for five minutes?" Simone asked. "Just the training part. Please?"

"Okay," Joseph agreed at last. "Just the training." He couldn't mess up a game that way.

*

"Welcome to roller hockey, Joseph!" Coach Eve said. "We'll start with some drills. See how you get on. You can take a rest whenever you want."

Joseph got in line for the first drill – hitting the puck around some cones.

It wasn't easy to skate and hit the puck at the same time, but he found he could do it if he really focused.

Five minutes went by, then ten. Joseph lost track of time as the training went on. "That's it for the drills!" shouted the coach. "Next, we'll play a training game!"

Joseph skated to the side of the rink.

"Why don't you join in the game?" Simone asked.

Joseph shook his head. "I'm tired," he fibbed.

"Will you come again next week?" Simone asked as his aunt drove Joseph home.

Joseph thought back to his time on the rink. It hadn't been that bad. And he hadn't fallen over!

"Maybe," he said.

*

At school on Monday, Philippa asked Joseph what he did at the weekend.

"Not much," he said, not saying anything about roller hockey.

"We lost our football game," Philippa complained. "We didn't even score one goal!"

At lunchtime, he told his mates he couldn't play football today. He'd prefer to stay inside doing homework than get teased by his mates for being rubbish!

CHAPTER 2

On Saturday, Simone and her mum came to pick Joseph up for roller-hockey training. Simone grinned at Joseph. "I'm so glad you said yes!" she said. "I've been thinking about the training all week!"

Joseph smiled back. Simone was always so positive – unlike his mates at school!

They started with drills again, and today, Joseph found it easier to skate and hit the puck at the same time.

"That's it!" Coach Eve called to Joseph. "You're getting the hang of it."

Like last week, they had a training game after the drills. And just like last week, Joseph sat on the bench.

Coach Eve looked around at him. "Are you sure you don't want to play?"

"No thanks!" Joseph said. But did he? It *did* look like so much fun, and Simone had explained all the rules to him in the car.

In the evenings after school that week, Joseph found loads of roller-hockey videos online.

On Wednesday, he called Simone to ask if he could come to training again.

He still didn't think he'd play in a game, but he loved skating around the rink, even just doing drills over and over.

*

Joseph avoided playing football at lunchtimes nearly all week, but there was no saying no to Jake on Friday.

"We need you to make up the numbers!" Jake said. *That's the only reason*, thought Joseph.

It was a disaster. Joseph didn't score an own goal, but he was supposed to be marking a winger. The winger did all these fantastic tricks to get past him. The rest of the players found it funny – even some on Joseph's side!

Joseph was so grumpy on Friday afternoon, he nearly called Simone after school to tell her he wasn't coming to roller hockey. But she'd sounded so happy when he'd spoken to her in the week that something stopped him.

CHAPTER 3

"Right, everyone, we have the semi-final of the cup next week, so today's training is really important!" Coach Eve said when they arrived at the rink on Saturday.

Simone hadn't said a thing to him about a semi-final! The coach wanted them to play a full training game before next week.

"Why don't you have a go today?" Coach Eve said to Joseph.

He shook his head.

He might have joined in if today's training game wasn't so important, but he didn't want to mess it up.

Like the last time, Joseph sat on the bench, tapping his feet. He followed the game, cheering on the players. When someone made a mistake, he thought about how he might have played it if he'd been on the rink.

At half-time, Simone sat down beside him. "Come on, Joseph, you've got to give it a try. I don't mind coming off for you!"

Coach Eve swung around. "What do you think, Joseph?"

"Um ..." Joseph began. He did really want to get back on the rink.

"We'll take that as a yes!" said Simone before Joseph could complain.

He was put on the wing and soon found himself speeding up and down the right-hand side.

Then the puck came zooming at him. Joseph looked up. The goalkeeper, Deven, was off his line, but Joseph didn't dare try a shot.

He sent the puck over to the left-hand side. Sita collected it and slid it into the goal.

She skated back and gave Joseph a high five.

Joseph smiled, proud of himself. He was doing okay!

At the end of the game, Simone begged him to come to the semi-final. "It's okay, I won't make you play!" she said.

"But I might!" said Coach Eve with a wink.

Joseph couldn't say no. And he really wanted to be there to cheer everyone on.

"All right," he said.

CHAPTER 4

"Did you see the big football game on TV on Saturday?" Jake asked at school on Monday.

Joseph was feeling so good, he told Jake what really happened.

"No, I was playing roller hockey," he said. "With my cousin, Simone."

Jake scrunched up his nose. "What's that? It can't be as good as football!"

"I've never even heard of it!" said Philippa, coming over. "Are you sure you didn't make it up?"

Joseph shook his head and said no more. There was no point.

He told himself not to be bothered about what his so-called mates said.

The week dragged by, but at last it was Saturday. "You were good last week, Joseph. I mean it," Simone told him when they arrived at the rink.

He smiled. "Thanks," he said as he glided along the rink. He never felt like this playing football. He wasn't bothered if his mates at school hadn't heard of roller hockey.

Joseph sat beside Coach Eve as the game began and she pointed out different tactics to Joseph as they played. "You can gain a lot from being on the bench," she said. "But one day I hope you'll play!"

It was 2-2 with just five minutes to go. Joseph tapped his feet on the ground nervously.

Simone picked up the puck after their opponents missed a shot. She blazed down the right wing, ducking around

defenders. At last, the other team seemed to be getting tired.

She looked up, but Joseph could see there was no one free to pass to. Simone made to shoot from her left side, but spun the puck and hit from the right, tricking the goalkeeper.

The entire bench jumped up as the goal went in.

They were in the final!

CHAPTER 5

The next Saturday came around fast. "It's final day!" Simone shouted as she and her mum arrived to pick up Joseph.

"Sophie and Justin are sick with a bug," Coach Eve told them when they arrived. "We have just the right amount for a team!"

Joseph looked around, panicking. He counted six of them, and they needed five on the rink. Phew – for a minute he thought he might have to play!

*

At the beginning of the second half, Simone yelped as she tried to spin around a defender.

She fell to the ground, shouting, "I've hurt my foot!"

Coach Eve turned to look at Joseph. "Can you play? I won't make you, but it seems like Simone can't carry on."

Joseph's entire body shook. He blinked and told himself not to panic. He couldn't let the team down.

He nodded slowly.

Coach Eve patted him on the back. "Thanks, Joseph. Believe in yourself!"

Joseph's legs didn't stop trembling as he got up from the bench. But as he glided on to the rink, he felt better.

Then he saw some kids passing by dressed in a very familiar football kit ... The kid at the front turned around and Joseph saw him clearly. It was Jake!

Jake's mouth dropped open when he saw Joseph.

He turned and poked Philippa who was next to him, giggling.

Oh no. This was just what he needed!

But Joseph couldn't run away – he'd just been put on to play.

He put Jake and Philippa out of his mind and skated over to mark an opponent. She had been hitting lots of shots and maybe Joseph could stop that.

He sped around the rink, but the other team were hard to defend against.

Sita took a shot from the halfway line, but it was saved by the goalkeeper and the puck pinged back into their half.

One of their opponents chased it, but she hit the puck badly and it skidded towards Joseph.

Joseph looked up, dinking the puck left and right. The goalkeeper came out of the goal, rushing towards him. He slid to the right, past the keeper, and stroked the puck into the back of the net.

Goal! His first goal!

His team crowded around him as the referee called for the end of the game.

They'd won! And Joseph had scored the winning goal!

The sound of cheering filled the room.

Joseph smiled, letting it all sink in.

"Hey," said someone behind him. Joseph looked around, and there were Jake and Philippa.

He groaned inside, waiting for them to tease him about playing a rubbish sport.

"Okay, so you've never heard of roller hockey," Joseph said, before they could say a thing, "but I'm not bothered if you think it's rubbish. I like it."

Jake's mouth gaped open. "We don't think it's rubbish. It looks like a lot of fun. And you're brilliant at it!"

"I'm sorry if we've been mean at school," Jake said. "You've hardly played football with us lately."

"Yes," added Philippa. "I was sad that you might have felt left out."

"I did a bit," Joseph admitted. "But I'm okay with not playing football. Just don't make me!"

"Deal," Jake said. "And we can still do other things together."

"Mates?" Philippa said.

"Mates," Joseph said with a smile, before turning back to celebrate with his team.

Chat about the book

1 Go to Chapter 5. How did Simone hurt her foot?

2 Read page 9. Why do you think Joseph lost track of the time?

3 Simone pestered Joseph to give roller hockey a go. What does 'pestered' mean?

4 Go to pages 14 and 15. Find 3 ways that show Joseph didn't enjoy playing football on Friday at school.

5 How does Joseph feel at the start and end of the story? What is different?

6 Were Jake and Philippa good friends to Joseph? What would you have done if you were Joseph?